THE TOMB OF THE BOY KING

Tutankhamen

Lord Carnarvon

Howard Carter

Lady Evelyn

Abdul Ali

JOHN FRANK PICTURES BY TOM POHRT

FRANCES FOSTER BOOKS · FARRAR STRAUS GIROUX · NEW YORK

For Matthew —J.F.
For Carrie —T.P.

Library of Congress Cataloging-in-Publication Data
Frank, John.
    The tomb of the boy king / John Frank ; pictures by Tom Pohrt.
        p.   cm.
    Summary: Tells, in rhyming text, the story of Howard Carter's efforts to find
Tutankhamen's tomb and of what he did discover in the Valley of the Kings.
    ISBN 0-374-37674-3
    1. Tutankhamen, King of Egypt——Tomb——Juvenile literature. 2. Carter,
Howard, 1874-1939——Juvenile literature. [1. Tutankhamen, King of Egypt
——Tomb. 2. Carter, Howard, 1874-1939.] 1. Pohrt, Tom, ill. II. Title.
DT87.5.F7   2001   99-27597

MEDITERRANEAN SEA

Rosetta
Alexandria

Cairo
Memphis

NILE RIVER

SINAI

RED SEA

Valley of the Kings • Karnak
• Luxor (Thebes)

EGYPT

PROLOGUE

A gold moon rose beyond the cliffs
and lured the robbers from their lair,
as sunset's last light bled upon
the sacred desert grave site where

the boy king, Tutankhamen, lay
surrounded by his treasure hoard,
protected by a curse, some say,
as dangerous as a sharpened sword.

He died at age eighteen; a court
official, some suspect, turned foe,
and crept behind him silently
and dealt his head a crushing blow.

His subjects thought his spirit would
return to life while in the grave,
and each day journey far away,
then back at night, when it would crave

the comfort of his body——which
would lie forever, mummified——
and all the splendid riches that
his mourners buried by his side.

But thieves could smell the scent of gold.
Now, hidden in the shades of dusk
that spread across the valley floor
as evening shed its twilight husk,

they moved with catlike stealth, alert
to every warning sight and sound,
and neared the spot where sixteen stairs
reached deep beneath the desert ground . . .

Some thirty centuries later, a
determined archaeologist
named Howard Carter clutched a worn-
out map of Egypt in his fist.

Since nineteen hundred seventeen
he'd combed the Valley of the Kings,
pursuing treasure that he hoped
stayed hid from robbers' ravagings—

the fortune Tutankhamen, king,
was buried with inside a tomb,
to savor in the afterlife
when born again from death's dark womb.

A rich friend, Lord Carnarvon, paid
the bills for Carter's costly quest,
but then, in nineteen twenty-two,
decided he should not invest

a penny more upon a search
that had, for years, borne no great find.
The stubborn archaeologist
resolved to change Carnarvon's mind,

and, seated in Carnarvon's home
(an English castle—stately, old),
he spoke his most convincing words,
the map of Egypt now unrolled.

"To hire a crew of men," he said,
"to labor in the desert sun
where nests of poisonous snakes abound
is not a task that's cheaply done.

"And there's one place we've not yet searched
along this portion of the Nile.
I'm certain that's where treasure waits.
No scorpion, snake, or crocodile

"will keep me from this one last dig.
And if we locate riches, fame
will follow you throughout the world:
the find will honor your good name!"

Carnarvon rubbed his chin, then said,
"I'll pay the bills one season more";
and Carter booked his passage back
by train and ship to Egypt's shore.

Once back in Egypt, Carter was
met shortly by his servant, who
had brought with him another man,
the foreman of the digging crew.

The two grabbed Carter's baggage, which
included, to their great surprise,
a pet canary in a cage.
Enchantment lit the foreman's eyes.

"A golden bird——what fortune! May
it guide us to the tomb!" he said.
Abdul Ali, the servant, cast
a nervous glance and shook his head,

and mumbled something to himself
about an "ancient mummy's curse"
and "letting pharaohs rest in peace"
and someone "riding in a hearse."

But Carter knew he'd need more than
the flutter of a bird's gold wings
to move the tons of rock and sand,
inside the Valley of the Kings,

that hid King Tutankhamen's tomb.
His crew began to excavate
a site of ancient workmen's huts;
they dug and sweat and hauled their weight

in broken rock a hundred times
each day, it seemed. And once again
it looked as if they'd wasted time
on Carter's wild-goose chase, but then . . .

a water boy, while kicking at
the earth to hollow out a spot
to set a jar in, felt his foot
strike something hard—a stone, he thought.

But as he scuffed away more dirt
a space appeared, of lighter hues;
he ran to tell the foreman, who,
in turn, told Carter of the news.

With Carter in the lead, the crew
grabbed picks and hoes and gathered round,
and cleared away the earth atop . . .
a stairway reaching underground.

Its stretch of steps was cut in rock,
and led them to an ancient door
whose face still wore a sacred seal
from thirty centuries past or more.

The door was built from blocks of stone,
its seal stamped with a strange design
that Egypt's priests gave noble dead:
a jackal with its captives, nine,

aligned in threes, upon bent knees,
their arms behind them tightly bound—
the workers stared in silent awe . . .
Whose grave was this that they had found?

Much rock and sand still hid from view
the ancient doorway's lower half,
but Carter made the workers halt
so he could send by telegraph

a message to Carnarvon's home,
inviting him to come and stay
and see the opening of the door—
and wired the telegram next day.

When Carter came home late that night,
exhausted from his long hard week,
Abdul Ali——awaiting him,
upset——began at once to speak.

"A cobra killed the bird," he cried,
"because it led us to the tomb!"
He held out, in his trembling hand,
the remnants of a golden plume.

"That's superstition," Carter scoffed.
The servant's voice grew cold with fright.
"Disturb the tomb no more," he warned,
then turned and vanished in the night.

But Carter let the matter drop——
for time and time again he'd heard
these rumors of a mummy's curse——
and thought no more about the bird,

except as an amusing tale——
"A curse, indeed!"——to get a laugh
once Lord Carnarvon showed up in
reply to Carter's telegraph.

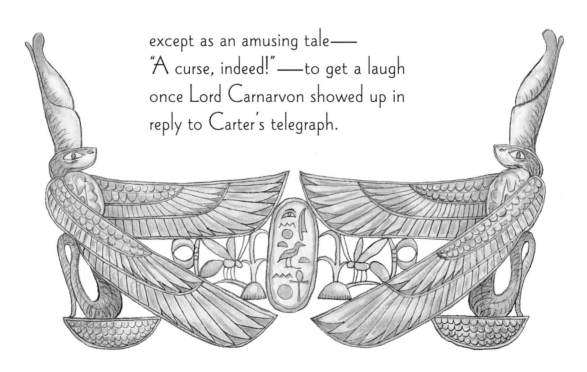

When Carter's friend arrived at last
(along with Lady Evelyn——"Eve"——
his daughter, who was eager to
observe a dig that might retrieve

a priceless piece of Egypt's past),
the crew began its work once more,
unearthing the remaining rock
that hid a portion of the door

until they'd cleared it all away.
Then Carter, with his guests in tow,
walked down those sixteen ancient steps
that reached into the dark below,

and knelt to read the lower seals.
His guests drew back to give him room.
They held their breath, and Carter spoke:
"We've found King Tutankhamen's tomb!"

Carnarvon and his daughter cheered.
A glance from Carter made them stop:
the smile had vanished from his face
as quickly as a water drop

upon a scorching desert rock.
He leaned against the limestone wall
and said, "Just look. There, on the door—
the robbers were here, after all."

He pointed to a plaster patch:
the thieves had likely come to steal
the loot by tunneling through the door;
the hole was mended with a seal

a king's officials must have made
once they'd found out about the theft—
and Carter knew, now, in the tomb
there probably was nothing left.

Poor Carter. All his lofty dreams
to stand apart in history—
to be remembered as the man
who honored archaeology

by prying the boy king's treasure free—
were quickly crumbling like a cake
of desert dirt. Frustration rose
and struck him like a vicious snake.

The *years* he'd squandered clawing through
those miles of blistering desert land!
The seas of sweat his pores had spilled!
The choking breaths of dust and sand!

For what! Yet one more foolish jaunt?
The history books were full of those!
(And so were children's fairy tales—
as emperor dressed in see-through clothes

was how *he'd* be remembered now:
"There *was* no treasure," they'd all say.
"It must have been a mere mirage
brought on by too much sun one day.")

But Carter had not come this far
to quit; if nothing else, he'd see
the inside of the ancient tomb,
though empty it was bound to be.

He called his crew to bring their tools,
and led the breaking of the door
until he had an opening,
behind which stretched a corridor,

and cleared more rubble, rock by rock,
till to a second door he came,
and through this one he chipped a hole
and shone a candle's sputtering flame . . .

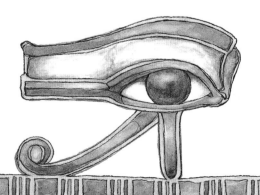

Three thousand years of darkness yawned
behind that tiny flickering light—
and Carter, staring with pupils wide,
stood stunned before a wondrous sight:

three golden couches shaped like beasts,
and under one a golden throne
(its arms two serpents, winged and crowned,
its back inlaid with glass and stone),

and calcite vases, finely carved,
and painted caskets, beds, and chairs,
and two wood statues, life-sized, stern,
whose golden eyes bore warning glares.

Excitement quickened Carter's heart.
While praying what the robbers stole
did not amount to much at all,
he chiseled out a larger hole,

and Eve climbed through, with Carter, Lord
Carnarvon, and an aide behind.
In disbelief they searched the room,
more riches dazzling each one's mind—

long silver trumpets, walking staffs,
and parts of golden chariots,
and wood and ivory boxes filled
with necklaces and amulets,

and cups and bowls, and urns and jugs,
and beaded sandals, tasseled belts,
cosmetic jars, gold sequins, and
a cloak made out of leopard pelts.

Electric lights were soon brought in,
and Lord Carnarvon, searching, found
an open space within a wall;
and, hands and knees upon the ground,

he peered inside . . . a second room . . .
piled waywardly with baskets, stools,
more boxes, vases, beds, and chairs,
and wooden game boards, metal tools,

and jars for oil, and jars for wine,
and bracelets, collars, pendants, rings,
and bows and arrows, swords of bronze,
and boomerangs and linen slings——

the thieves must not have gotten much!
Afraid, perhaps, that guards were near,
they must have sacked the rooms for gold
and hurried from the tomb in fear.

Carnarvon summoned Carter to
the wake left by the robbers' squall,
while Evelyn, still exploring, ran
her hand along the northern wall

behind the statues standing watch—
then froze in place and fixed her eyes
upon a plastered area . . .
about a doorway's shape and size.

"There must be one more room!" Eve cried.
"The spot right here must be a door!"
But when they chiseled through the wall,
they came upon not one room more

but two!——two chambers guarded by
a jackal god in gold and black,
which lay atop a gilded shrine,
with linen draped across his back.

And in the smaller of the rooms
were chests of ivory, quartz, and wood,
and yet another wrought in gold
around which goddess statues stood,

protecting with their outstretched arms
an alabaster shrine within,
which held four tiny coffins, glass
tattooed upon their golden skin.

And jewelry hid within the chests——
more silver, gold, and inlaid stones
(carnelian, turquoise, amethyst,
green feldspar, quartz——in brilliant tones)——

as did a host of statuettes——
the pharaoh posed with spears and rods;
and, wearing wreaths of leaves and grain,
two dozen carved Egyptian gods;

and hundreds of *ushabtis*——small
carved figures holding crooks and flails——
and all about were model boats
with rigging, oars, and linen sails.

But waiting first beyond the door,
and reaching nearly wall to wall,
there stood, inside the larger room,
the most astounding find of all:

four shrines——one hid within the next——
and in the fourth a vault of stone,
and in that vault a coffin lay,
on which a golden cobra shone;

the coffin held two coffins more——
eight chests in all, a grand disguise
(like Chinese boxes, large to small,
each swallowing the next in size).

It took him months to coax the chests
all, one by one, to free their hold,
but Carter finally reached the end:
a coffin made of solid gold.

And there inside, in mummy wrap,
his jeweled arms across his breast,
a mask of gold upon his head . . .
King Tutankhamen lay at rest.

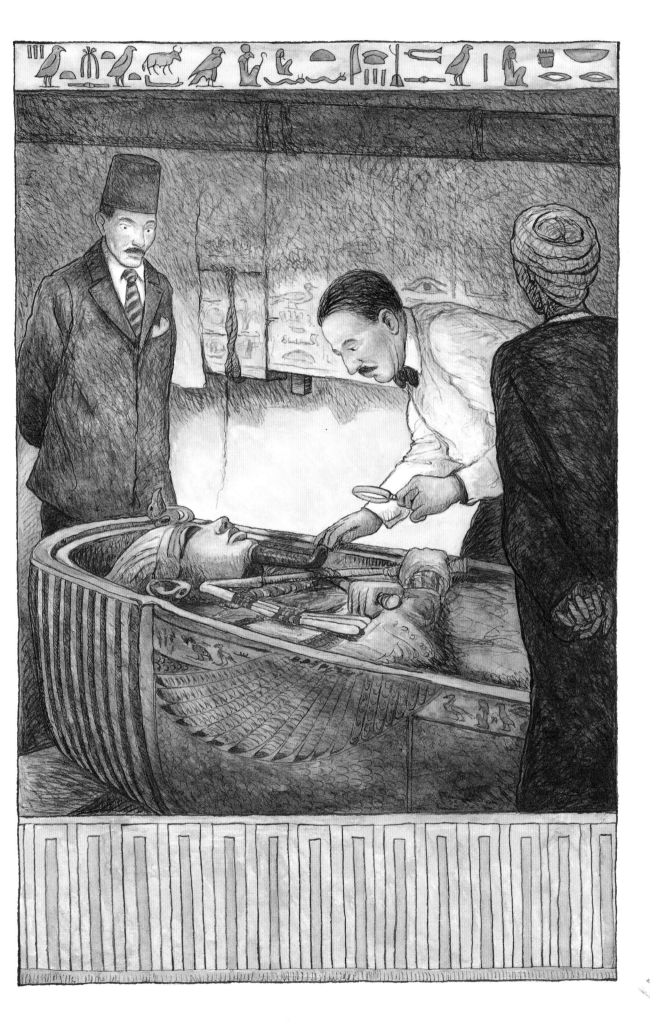

Before long, Carter's triumph had
become the talk of everyone;
the public spotlight shone on him
as brightly as the desert sun.

Across the world the headlines hailed
the man who ventured underground
and brought back from the ancient past
the greatest treasure ever found.

And what became of Carter's friend?
Alas, Carnarvon met his doom
before the final coffin's lid
was lifted off inside the tomb.

Some claim he died of fever brought
about by a mosquito bite
that got infected while he shaved—
and nicked the wound—at home one night.

And some insist we'll never know
what caused Carnarvon's tragic end.
But some, more superstitious, say
that Carter's close and loyal friend,

who paid for the expensive dig
with contributions from his purse,
should have, instead, paid heed to one
pet bird—and Tutankhamen's curse.

EPILOGUE

Tutankhamen was only nine years old when he became king of Egypt. But it's unlikely he ever had much power. Historians believe a high-ranking government official named Ay and a general named Horemheb did most of the ruling during the young king's reign. When Tutankhamen died, Ay took the throne.

We have very few facts about Tutankhamen himself. Some of what we do know about him came from autopsies—medical examinations of the dead body. Through careful study, doctors were able to estimate Tutankhamen's standing height (just under five and a half feet) as well as the age at which he died (about eighteen). But X rays of the king's head proved puzzling. They showed a stray fragment of bone lodged beneath his skull. How did it get there?

One guess was that the fragment had broken off during mummification. In ancient Egypt, embalmers (the "mummy makers") would use a long metal hook to remove a dead person's brains through the nostrils. So it seemed reasonable to conclude that the piece of bone had come from the king's nose. But further examination proved that conclusion wrong, and a more likely explanation took its place: the fragment had come from the skull itself, perhaps as a result of a blow to the head. This fueled the belief that Tutankhamen had been murdered. Who, though, would have had a reason to kill him? Many believe Ay might have—so he could take over as king. But we have no way of knowing with any certainty.

One thing we can say for sure is that Tutankhamen was given one of the most elaborate burials in history. Howard Carter and his associates found over five thousand objects in the king's tomb. It took Carter ten more years to finish cataloguing all those artifacts and to prepare them, piece by piece, for safe transport to the Cairo Museum. Unfortunately, Lord Carnarvon wasn't around to see him complete the job.

Which brings up another question: how did Carnarvon really die? The public was told he got blood poisoning after accidentally cutting a mosquito bite with his razor. The blood poisoning, it was said, led to pneumonia—and that's what was officially listed on Carnarvon's death certificate as the cause of death.

But some troubling coincidences remain unexplained. At the recorded late-night moment Carnarvon died in a Cairo hotel, his family dog—back in England—let out a bloodcurdling howl and dropped dead, too. That same instant, the lights blacked out all over Cairo. And perhaps oddest of all, the first autopsy of the mummy revealed a wound on Tutankhamen's left cheek—in precisely the same spot where Carnarvon's cheek received the mosquito bite that led to his death.